A Brother the Size of Me

A Brother
the Size of Me

by

HELEN DOSS

Illustrated by Robert Patterson

Boston LITTLE, BROWN AND COMPANY Toronto

*Published simultaneously in Canada
by Little, Brown & Company (Canada) Limited*

PRINTED IN THE UNITED STATES OF AMERICA

Contents

A Brother the Size of Me

1. The New Boy

DONNY was sitting on the front porch, patting Rufus, his red cocker spaniel. He watched his mother take an airmail letter from their mailbox.

"This is from that orphanage I wrote to," his mother said, ripping open the envelope. "I wonder what they have to say?"

Donny jumped up, and his blue eyes were popping

with excitement. "Am I going to get a new brother? Am I?"

Mother unfolded the letter, and Donny thought she would never finish reading it.

"Tell me what it says!" Donny begged. "Have they got a boy?"

"Yes, they have a boy that we can adopt," Mother said, turning to the second page. She smiled at Donny. "They have a little boy who is Japanese and Mexican. His name is Timmy —"

"Is he the right size of me?" Donny asked eagerly. "Is he?"

Mother shook her head. "No, he's —" She looked at the letter again. "As a matter of fact, he is just exactly a year younger than Rita. That would make him two years younger than Teddy —"

Four children, all smaller than Donny, pushed through the screen door onto the porch. There were three girls and one boy, all about the same size.

"Who is two years younger than me?" slim little Teddy wanted to know. His skin was brown, and he had big brown eyes.

4

"Yes, and who is one year littler than *me?*" the smallest girl asked. Rita was slim and brown-skinned, too. She had black, dancing eyes. Her hair was black and shiny, as black and shiny as her patent-leather slippers which she wore to Sunday School on Sundays.

"Yes, Mama, *who* is?" the other two girls wanted to know. They had their arms around each other. Susan was blond and blue-eyed, like her big brother Donny. Chubby little Laura had a round face, with brown eyes and silky-straight brown hair.

"We're talking about adopting us a new brother," Donny said. "From the orphanage Mama wrote to."

"Hurray!" his four small brothers and sisters shouted. They started jumping up and down like Mexican jumping beans.

Finally they stopped, and Teddy asked, "How old is the new brother?"

"One year younger than Rita, and two years younger than *you*," Donny said disgustedly. "That's what we were talking *about*."

"Oh, boy!" Teddy said. "Can he sleep in my room, with me?"

"If we decide to adopt this little Timmy," Mother said, "I suppose he can sleep with you, Teddy."

"Oh, boy!" Teddy chuckled, his brown eyes sparkling.

"Will you really decide?" Susie asked.

"To dopple that boy?" Rita added.

"Not *dopple*," Donny said. "*Adopt.* That means when a mama and a daddy bring home a boy, or a girl, to be their own. And the judge asks, Will you love this child just like he was born to you? And the parents say, *Yes.* So the judge says, *Now you're adopted.* That's what you were, and that's what I was, adopted."

"*I* was adopted, too," Teddy said proudly.

"Us, too," Laura and Susie chimed in, together.

"Well, I rather think we should adopt this little Timmy, too," Mother said. "And I'm sure your daddy will agree."

"Hurray, hurray!" Donny's little brother and sisters shouted, even louder than before. They started jumping up and down again. Then they all jumped off the front porch and raced around to the back yard, whooping and hollering like wild Indians.

Mother put her arm around Donny. "You see, this little Timmy is all alone, up there in that orphanage. He doesn't have any daddy and mama to take care of him. He *needs* a family like ours."

"I suppose so," Donny sighed. He sounded downhearted.

Mother gave him a hug. "So I think we ought to adopt him, even if he *isn't* just your size. Don't you?"

"I suppose so," Donny said. Then he burst out, "But Teddy, and Laura, and Susie — and — and Rita, they all got each other! They are all the same size, and they all play together. But *I* don't have anybody my size to play with!"

"Your little brother and sisters will be happy to have you play with them," Mother said, "I'm sure."

"Yes, but they are just simply too little and too silly," Donny said. "They don't understand *my* kind of games."

7

"They will get older." Mother smiled. She put the letter in her apron pocket and went back into the house.

Donny scuffed across the front yard. His house was out in the country, right next door to the little white-painted country church with the steeple where his father was the minister.

Donny scuffed his way around the front of the church, dragging the toes of his shoes on the gravel driveway, his hands in his pockets.

On the other side of the church, Donny looked around. Nobody had followed him, except his dog. His younger brother and sisters were nowhere in sight.

Donny parted the bushes, and crawled on his hands and knees into his hide-out hole, under the church. Rufus followed Donny in, and stood beside him.

Donny put his arm around Rufus. His eyes were not used to the dimness yet, so he couldn't see his dog's stubby tail wagging. But he could feel it. The whole furry, warm body was wiggling. Donny

leaned his head against Rufus, and the dog sat down, quiet.

"Grownups don't understand," Donny said. "*Your brother and sisters will play with you when they get older!* That's what Mama says. But when they get older, I'll get older, too. So they'll *always* be littler than me."

Rufus started wagging his tail again. It stirred up the soft loose dirt under the church.

"Grownups don't understand," Donny said, "but *you* do." He sat quiet for a while, and Rufus was quiet, too. "It wasn't too bad when I was little and Mama and Daddy went out and adopted those two baby girls. Laura and Susie — they were okay. Then, when I asked Mama to adopt a brother the size of me, who did they find?"

Rufus wagged his tail and stirred up more dust, so that Donny sneezed.

Donny found a handkerchief in his pocket and blew his nose. "They found Teddy, that's who they found. Sure, Teddy was okay, too. But he was just the same age as my little sisters, so *that* was no help. So the next year I asked Mama if we could adopt just one more. So then who did they find?"

Rufus wagged his tail vigorously, and Donny sneezed again.

"They found Rita, that's who," Donny said. "She was even littler than all the rest! And now we're going to get a new boy, even littler than *that*."

Rufus licked Donny's cheek with his warm tongue. Donny hugged his dog.

"I'm sure glad I got *you*, anyway," he said. "You're the only one who understands me. You're the very best thing I own, in this whole, whole world!"

The next week, while his mother was packing her suitcase, Donny had an idea.

"When you get up there, to that orphanage," he said, "could you sort of look around? For a bigger boy, I mean?" Donny scratched his blond head. "I mean, if you found one the size of me, couldn't you trade him off for that Timmy, and bring the bigger one home, instead?"

His mother laughed and hugged him. "You certainly want a boy your size more than anything, don't you?"

11

Donny nodded, and he had to blink hard so the tears wouldn't come. "Yes. More than *anything.*"

Mother kissed him. "Well, I promise I will look around when my train gets to the orphanage. I still want to bring that little Timmy home. But if I happen to find a boy there your size — one who doesn't have any family — I'll see if I can bring him home, too."

The sunshine came back into Donny's face.

"But you must not get your hopes too high," his mother warned him.

When his mother left, Donny's hopes sailed as high as a jet airplane. Donny simply could not help himself. All the time his mother was gone, he kept saying to himself, "I *hope* she finds a boy the same size as me! I hope, I hope, I *hope!*"

At last came the day when Daddy said, "Pile into the car, children! We're off to the station, to bring Mother and Teddy home!" Teddy had gone along with Mother, to be company for Timmy on the trip home.

The children climbed into the car. Daddy smiled as

13

he started up the car. "And today we'll bring your new brother, Timmy, home, too."

On the way, Donny's three little sisters sang songs and bounced around in the back seat of the family station wagon.

"I'm going to teach that Timmy how to collect bugs," Rita said, pushing her black hair out of her eyes. She held a glass jar tightly with her small brown fingers. The lid of the jar had holes punched in it. "I've got him a present. It's a big green beetle, to start his collection."

"Do you suppose he bites?" Laura asked, her chubby face worried.

"Not *my* bug," Rita said indignantly.

"No, I mean the new brother," Laura said.

Susie shook her blond head. "Our new brother wouldn't bite."

"Well, some little boys do," Laura said darkly. She was beginning to look jealous.

Donny sat quietly in the front seat, next to his father. "You don't have much to say," Daddy smiled, watching the road as he drove. "Aren't you excited?"

14

Donny grinned up at his father. "Yep. I guess I am!" But he didn't tell his father what he was *really* excited about. He was having a hard time waiting until they got to the station. Maybe his mother would get off the train with a boy just his size!

They finally reached the station.

"Let's all stay together," Daddy said, as they piled out of the car. He took the hands of Susie and Laura. "Rita, you hold Donny's hand, so nobody gets lost."

They waited on the station platform, looking down the tracks.

"I see a train coming!" Donny said.

The engine rushed down the tracks, getting closer and louder. It ground to a stop, spitting steam and screeching. People climbed off, but no Mama. No brother the size of Donny.

"That's not your mother's train," Daddy said. "It will be along soon."

It seemed like a long, long time. Then Donny heard a whistle in the distance, and another train was pounding down the tracks.

15

"Stand back," Daddy said. "I think this is the one."

Donny was so excited he could hardly stand still.

The train screeched and hissed, and grumbled to a stop. The conductors and the brakemen and the porters jumped down, and set up the little stools by the steps. Then they started helping people down the steps.

"I don't see Mama," Laura said.

"Yes, there she is, there she is!" Susie shouted. "And there's Teddy, and they got a little boy by the hand!"

"That must be our Timmy," Daddy nodded. "He looks like a roly-poly little elf."

Donny looked. There were his mother and Teddy. Between them, holding on to their hands, was a chubby little boy. He was even smaller than Rita.

Donny looked at all the other passengers. There was no boy the size of him. There were no other children getting off the train.

"Mama, Mama!" Donny ran, and threw himself into

his mother's arms. He looked up into her face. He couldn't give up hope. He *couldn't*.

"Didn't you bring home a brother the size of me?" he asked.

His mother hugged him. "I wish I could, Donny. But you see, Timmy was the oldest boy they had."

Donny looked down at the little boy. Timmy stared at Donny with his big brown eyes, and hid behind Mama's skirt.

"He is a very lovable little boy," Mother said. "Let's go introduce him to Daddy and his new sisters."

Daddy took Timmy and threw him up into the air. Timmy chuckled, a deep, low chuckle that made everybody else laugh, too.

"I've got a bug for you," Rita said, holding out her glass jar. "You like bugs?"

"Yep." Timmy grinned. "I like bugs."

Susie smiled at her mother and father, and pointed to Timmy. "That boy's nice. I *like* him."

Laura scowled and backed away. "*I* don't," she said. "*I* think Mama ought to take him back."

17

Mother picked up Laura then, and kissed her. "You are just a bit jealous, honey, that's all. You'll get over it."

When they got home, everybody trooped into the house to show the new brother around.

Everybody except Donny. He slipped away, followed by Rufus. They went around the church, and crawled into Donny's hide-out. Donny put his arm around his dog and hugged him.

"Laura is the only one of the kids who has sense," Donny told Rufus. "That's what we really should do, send him back. That Timmy is just too little for this family."

Donny had to blink really fast now. It was hard to keep from crying, because he was that disappointed.

"All I asked for was just *one* boy the size of me," he told Rufus. "Grownups just don't understand."

His dog wagged his tail furiously. After a while, with the dust stirred up all around, Donny sneezed.

"I don't know what I'd do, if I didn't have *you* for my best friend," Donny whispered into the long, floppy ear.

Teddy   Susan   Timmy

Rita   Laura

Donny

2. The Surprise

AFTER Timmy had been in the family for a while, everybody loved him. Laura stopped being jealous — she discovered it was fun to help take care of her new little brother. Even Donny was glad that Timmy had come to live at their house.

"But there *still* isn't anybody for me to play with," Donny complained one night, after all the younger children had gone off to bed. "Can't we adopt *one more boy* — a brother the size of me?"

"That would be nice — " Mother began.

"But quite *impossible*," his father said. "We just simply cannot *afford* to have a bigger family. A minister, in a country church, doesn't make much money, you know."

"It wouldn't cost much," Donny pleaded. "I'll share my blankets and toys and my room, with a brother my size."

Daddy shook his head, and picked up his book. "We already have six children now. I think that is enough."

The next morning, after a breakfast of orange juice, hot oatmeal cooked with raisins, and a tall glass of milk, Donny went outside. He whistled for Rufus.

"It's Saturday, and no school," he told Rufus. "Let's go for a walk." They went out past the church, and started down the country road toward town.

"I wonder what I could do to earn some money?" Donny said to Rufus. "I'll bet if I could earn some money and give it to Daddy, then Daddy would think we could afford another boy."

Rufus trotted along beside Donny, his stubby tail wagging and his red tongue lolling out of his mouth.

They passed a cabin where an old man and an old lady lived. The old man had his whole front yard spaded up and neatly planted in a garden. Tiny shoots of early vegetables already were pushing through the ground.

Donny snapped his fingers, and Rufus looked up at him, expectantly.

"I've got it!" Donny said. "I'll grow a garden, and sell all the vegetables. What shall I plant first?"

They walked along, and soon they were in front of the country store. It was a general store, and there were groceries in the windows, and bolts of cloth, and overalls, and shiny tin milk pails.

A little girl came out of the store with her cheeks puffed out. She had a box of popcorn in her hand, and she was stuffing popcorn into her mouth.

"I've got it!" Donny said. "The first thing I plant will be *popcorn!*"

He ran all the way home. Rufus ran back and forth and around him, barking with excitement.

In his room, Donny took his piggy bank, and started shaking it over his bed. A nickel came out. Then a penny. At last a half dollar came out. Donny put the penny and the nickel back in the bank, and he put the half dollar in his pocket. He ran all the way back downtown, Rufus barking at his heels.

In the store, Donny told the man, "I'd like to buy some seeds."

The man took him to the back of the store and pointed to a big rack. Many seed packets were displayed, each with a brightly colored picture of a vegetable. The next rack had flower seeds.

"What kind of seeds did you have in mind?" the man asked.

Donny pointed to the vegetable rack. "Before I'm through with my garden, I'll probably raise some of everything you've got there." He took the half dollar out of his pocket. "Just for a starter, you can give me a big box of popcorn seed. You've got popcorn seed?"

"You bet I have." The man took a box from down

near the bottom of the rack. He put it in a sack, and took Donny's half dollar. Then he rang it up on the cash register, and gave Donny his change. Donny took his money and his sack and ran all the way home.

Back in his room, Donny dropped the change into his piggy bank. He patted the pig. "Pretty soon, when I sell my popcorn, old pig, you'll be so fat with money you'll bust. And then maybe Daddy will let me have a new brother, just my size!"

Rufus followed Donny out to the tool shed, where Donny found a spading fork. Donny dragged it out to a corner of the back yard and started digging.

After a while he got hot and tired, and sat down. Rufus came over and licked Donny's face, which was red and dripping. Donny wiped the perspiration from his forehead, and put his arm around Rufus.

"This is awfully hard work, trying to earn enough money for a brother," he told his dog. He sighed. "But it's worth it."

Donny's father came out and looked at Donny's hot red face. He looked at the clods of dirt Donny had spaded.

24

"I'm planting popcorn," Donny explained. He pulled the box out of his pocket. "Do you suppose I've got almost enough dug up to plant all this?"

Donny's father laughed. "You'll need a lot more than this, if you want to plant that whole big package."

Donny looked discouraged.

"I'll tell you what," his father said, picking up the spading fork. "You run to the tool shed and get the rake. I'll go ahead and spade up enough ground for you. *You* can chop it up fine, with the rake, and rake it smooth."

So Daddy spaded up a big piece of ground. Donny chopped the clods and raked it smooth. Then Daddy showed Donny how to mark his row, and how to plant his corn seeds.

That night, Donny came into the house for dinner, and he was more tired and hungry than he had been in a long time.

"That was sure work," he said, "but it was worth it." He was thinking how surprised his mother and father would be when he sold all the extra popcorn he grew.

26

He would put the money in their hands and say, "*Now* you can go get me that brother my size!"

Donny's father was talking to him.

"Planting your popcorn is only part of the job," his father was saying. "You have to keep the weeds chopped out. And you'll have to drag the hose over there whenever the ground gets dry. Corn cannot grow without water!"

Donny watered his garden every day for a week. Then he grew tired of waiting for the first sprouts to come through.

"Maybe I'd better start something else, while I'm waiting," he told Rufus. "I could buy some different seeds, but I'm afraid Daddy hasn't time to help me dig some more."

Donny leaned on the fence and looked over at the neighbor's yard. The lady next door was leaning over the gate of her chicken yard. She was throwing corn out of a pan. The chickens scratched the ground, pecking up the corn. Then the lady next door went into the hen house. When she came out, her pan was full of big white eggs.

27

Donny snapped his fingers and Rufus looked up, his stubby tail wagging.

"I've got it!" Donny said. "We'll raise *chickens*, too. Then any extra popcorn that we can't eat, or can't sell, won't go to waste. We'll give it to the chickens! Does that sound good?"

Rufus licked his chops.

Donny ran into his room, and shook all the money out of his pig. There weren't any more half dollars, but there were a few dimes and quarters, and a pile of pennies and nickels. It had taken him a long, long time to save this much.

He scooped up the money in his hands and went to look for his mother and father. He found them in the living room. Mother was all dressed up, and Daddy was handing her the car keys.

Donny held out his hands. "Look, is this enough money to buy some baby chickens? I want to earn some money, and —"

His mother was in a hurry to leave, and she wasn't really listening. "I have to hurry off to Santa Rosa for a dentist appointment," she said, "and some shopping.

You tell Daddy your problem, and then you can tell *me* after I come home."

"But if you're going to Santa Rosa, then I have to talk to you *now*," Donny said desperately. He held out his handful of money. "Would you buy me as many baby chicks as this much would buy?"

"Baby chicks?" Mother asked. "What on earth do you want with baby chicks?"

"I'll raise them," Donny said. "I can sell their eggs, all the extra ones we don't eat. And I'll feed them my extra popcorn. I'm liable to have a *bumper* crop."

"Oh, no," his mother started to say, "no chickens — "

Daddy took Donny's money, wrapped it in a piece of paper, and put it in Mother's purse. "Oh, go ahead and get him some. It will be good experience for him. *I* was raising my own chickens when I wasn't much older than that."

Donny could hardly wait until his mother came home that night. When she came in the front door, she held a big box, with holes all around it. The box was cheeping.

29

"My baby chicks, my baby chicks!" Donny shouted excitedly.

His mother set the box on the floor, and she was smiling.

"When you children are all through looking at Donny's surprise," she said, "then your daddy and I have another surprise for you." She gave Daddy a kiss. "I telephoned San Francisco while I was down there. We can go and get him tomorrow!"

But the children weren't listening to Mother. They were all crowded around Donny, as he took the lid off the box. It was full of little balls of yellow fuzz, all running on tiny legs and cheeping.

"These are mine," Donny said proudly. "I'm going to make a lot of money for us, when they are big, fat hens. Extra eggs for everybody, too."

"Can we hold one?" Teddy asked.

"If you're careful," Donny said.

Donny and Teddy each picked up a baby chick, and cuddled it in their hands. Then Timmy and the three little girls each picked up a chick, too.

"Soft," Rita said, holding a peeping chick against her cheek.

"We'd better put them back to bed now," Donny said, "before they get too tired." The children returned the chicks to the box, and Donny carefully put the lid back on.

"You can put the box on the kitchen stove tonight," his father said. "The pilot light will keep them warm. Maybe tomorrow I can help you make some kind of brooder for them."

"Not *tomorrow*," Mother said mysteriously. "You'll have to do that the next day. Tomorrow is the day we go into San Francisco, to get our wonderful surprise."

"Surprise?" Donny asked. "Is there another surprise?"

"Yes, what surprise?" all the younger children echoed.

"You tell them," Mother told Daddy, her eyes twinkling.

"We've found a new brother for you," Daddy said. "How would you like to have another boy in our family?"

Donny was so excited he forgot his chickens. "A new brother?" he shouted. "The size of me, the size of me?"

Mother shook her head. "That would be nice, too. But this is just a baby boy. He is two years younger than Timmy."

The next day was a busy one. Daddy helped Donny make a little pen for his chicks. He showed Donny how to fix their water and fill up the feeder. Then the whole family dressed in their Sunday clothes, and piled into the station wagon for the long trip to San Francisco.

It was almost dark when they finally arrived home. The new baby was in his basket, howling. He had cried and howled all the way home.

While Mama fed the baby, and put the younger children to bed, Daddy helped Donny gather up his fuzzy chicks and put them into their box. Then Daddy carried the box into the house. He told Donny he would put them over the pilot light on the stove, so they would keep warm.

Donny sat down on the back step. He leaned his elbows on his knees, and cupped his chin in his hands.

Rufus came up and pushed his cold nose against Donny's cheek. Donny put his arms around his dog's neck.

"Did you see my new brother?" Donny asked Rufus. "He's really just a baby." He sat, watching the first stars come out. Then he sighed. "I think my new chickens were the best surprise, don't you?"

Alex

3. Another Disappointment

DONNY'S new little brother was named Alex.

"Why does he have such narrow eyes when he laughs?" Donny asked. "Can he see very well, when they are almost shut?"

"He certainly can!" his father laughed. "Alex has Oriental eyes. You see he is mostly Japanese and Korean."

"Our family comes from all around the world, doesn't

it?" Donny said. "Teddy is Filipino and Spanish. And Laura is Filipino and Chinese and English. What am I?"

"You and Susie are various mixtures of European," Daddy said. "Just like your mother and me. But we are all *Americans*, our whole family. It is just our *ancestors* who lived all around the world."

"You could call us a hands-around-the-world family, couldn't you?" Donny said.

"Yes," his father smiled. "I think you could."

Alex turned out to be a happy little boy, once he got settled in the family. After a while Donny became very fond of him.

One day Donny was bouncing Alex on his lap, and Alex was laughing. Alex had a lovable little face, the color of butterscotch pudding. His dark eyes crinkled shut as he laughed. His black hair stood straight up on his head.

"Alex has a natural-born butcher haircut," Timmy observed.

"You mean a *butch*," Donny corrected. He bounced

Alex again, so that the little boy laughed some more. Donny looked at his mother, who was ironing his school shirts. "Do you know what, Mama?"

"No, what?" his mother asked.

"If Alex was my age, and if I had black hair, everybody would think that we was twins!"

"Everybody would think that we *were* twins," his mother corrected.

"Well, they would," Donny insisted.

But Donny didn't have very much time to spend with Alex. He was too busy trying to raise his chicks. He had to keep giving them fresh water. He had to keep their feeder pan full of chicken feed. Rufus always stood outside the pen, wagging his tail madly, when Donny was taking care of the chicks.

"I'm *still* going to try to make some money by raising these chickens," he told Rufus, as he went out of the pen and hooked the gate. He patted his dog. "They are so good at finding really *little* kids to adopt into this family, wouldn't you think they could find just *one* the right size of me?"

Rufus wagged his tail, and Donny hugged him. "Well, at least I've got you, old boy. You're the best friend I've got."

Then one day something happened.

Little Timmy opened the gate to Donny's chicken pen, and went in to see the chickens. He forgot to close the gate. All the little chicks went chirping out of the gate, and fluttered off in all directions.

Donny came around the corner of the house just then, with Rufus at his heels. There was Timmy, running back and forth, trying to shoo the chicks back into the pen. The chicks only scampered farther away.

"Help, help!" Donny hollered, running to the pen. "My chickens are running away!"

Teddy and the girls came rushing out of the house, and Daddy came running out of the church. Daddy shut the gate, and everybody tried to catch the scampering chicks. Donny caught two, and put them in the pen.

Rufus saw one fluttering across the back yard, and started after him.

"Go get him, boy!" Donny said. Then he crawled

under a stickery blackberry bush and clutched another chick in his hand.

When all the chickens they could find were gathered up, there were only eight in the pen.

"Where are the ones *you* caught, Rufus?" Donny asked his dog. Rufus wagged his tail.

"Daddy, look!" Rita cried. "Rufus has feathers growing out of his mouth!"

Donny looked, too. There was no doubt of it.

"I'm afraid Rufus didn't understand about the right way to catch chickens," Daddy said.

Donny swallowed hard. "Well, I guess I can't blame him. After all, he's a *bird* dog, isn't he?"

His father nodded. "Yes, but a good, well-trained bird dog won't harm the birds he catches. You'll have to keep a close watch on him, now that he's had a taste of chickens. He might try to get more."

Donny patted Rufus, and sadly pulled the feathers from the soft, velvety mouth. "I don't think he'll do it again, though."

Donny was wrong.

Two weeks later, he woke up and looked out of his

bedroom window. The pen was empty. Usually the chicks were clustered around the feeders and the water jar, having their breakfast. But no chicks were in sight.

Donny jumped into his clothes and rushed out through the kitchen. "Hey, Daddy," he shouted, "my chickens all disappeared!"

His father followed Donny out to the chicken pen, and little Timmy came running after them.

"Where did they go?" Donny cried out. "The gate is shut."

"Hey, look," Timmy said. He pointed to a big hole that went under the fence. "Somebody dug a hole, right under that fence."

"Something has dug into the pen," Daddy said, shaking his head, "and eaten up all your chicks. I'm afraid it was Rufus."

"Oh, no," Donny said, his face puckered up, "not *Rufus*. It *must* have been something else — a skunk, or — or maybe a coyote."

Just then the furry red cocker spaniel came bounding up, his long ears flapping as he ran. He sat down in front of Donny and wagged his stubby tail.

41

Donny looked at his dog. He could not believe what he saw. Rufus sat there, his big front paws muddy — *from digging!* And he had a couple of downy white chicken feathers clinging to his velvety mouth!

"Rufus!" Donny said, shocked. "How could you do that? You're a *bad, bad* doggie."

Rufus knew he was being scolded. He got up and walked a few slow steps away. His head hung down sadly. His long ears drooped almost to the ground. His stubby tail didn't stick straight out at a jaunty angle any more. It was pulled in tight and down, and it wasn't wagging.

"You hurt his feelings," Timmy said, rushing over to pat Rufus. "He looks too sad."

Donny shook his head. "But he did that, and he was my *friend.*"

Daddy nodded. "Rufus still is your friend. He didn't realize those were *your* chickens. He got a taste of chicken before, and thought they tasted mighty fine. So maybe he got hungry, and just decided to have another good chicken dinner."

"But I fed him last night," Donny said. "Same as always."

"Don't *you* ever have the urge to eat between meals?" smiled Daddy.

Donny grinned back. "Yes, I guess so. I guess Rufus wasn't doing any worse than me when I raid the pantry." His face clouded up. "But it still hurts my feelings."

Daddy put his arm around Donny's shoulders. "I know this was a great disappointment, after all your hard work. But don't be too hard on your Rufus. You know, he's a pretty good dog, down underneath."

Timmy stopped patting Rufus, and squatted down. He looked underneath. Then he stood up.

"I think he looks better on the top," he said.

Donny began to laugh. "That's not what Daddy meant, funny boy."

Donny whistled to Rufus. Rufus looked up, and his tail started to wag, slowly, hopefully.

"It's okay, Rufus, old doggie," Donny said, leaning over and holding out his arms. "I guess you didn't mean to ruin my project, did you?"

The cocker's tail wagged furiously now. He came on the run, throwing himself against his master so enthusiastically he almost knocked Donny over.

Donny sat down, and Rufus jumped into his master's lap, licking his face.

After breakfast, Donny and Rufus went for a walk, down along the creek. Donny threw sticks into the shallow water. Rufus paddled out to get them. He brought them back dripping, and dropped them into Donny's lap.

"You're a good dog, Rufus," Donny said, "even if you *did* make a mistake. I forgive you, because I make mistakes, too, don't I?"

He put his arm around his dog, and his voice was sad. "But now that you've eaten up all my chickens, how am I going to earn enough money — so we can afford another brother?"

Suddenly he snapped his fingers. "My popcorn! All this time, I forgot about my popcorn!"

It was starting to rain as Donny hurried home. The drops pattered down on his shoulders and his blond hair, and one dropped on his nose. Donny paid no attention to the raindrops, because his mind was on something else.

He was disappointed when he looked at his garden. The little cornstalks drooped. Their leaves were turning yellow. They were almost choked out by the weeds.

"Daddy warned me to keep it watered," Donny said sadly. "It's all drying up, all my popcorn." He shook his head. "What a waste."

Rufus wagged his tail again.

Donny snapped his fingers. "I'll do it! Maybe we can save the crop!" He ran to the side of the house and screwed the hose to the faucet. Then he dragged the nozzle end over to the garden, ran back, and turned the water on.

There was a flash of lightning, followed by a distant rumble of thunder. The raindrops came down, thicker and faster.

Donny paid no attention. He was too busy watering his garden.

A window came up in the house. Daddy leaned out, and called, "Donny!"

45

Donny was too busy. He did not hear anything.

"Hey, there — *Donny!*" Daddy shouted, until Donny looked around. "What in heaven's name are you doing out there, in all the rain?"

"I'm watering my garden," Donny said. "So the popcorn will grow."

His father shook his head. "Your popcorn is *dead*. Turn off that hose, and come in here, out of the rain."

Donny turned off the hose and scuffed back to the house. He stood on the back porch, watching the rain pour down. He looked very, very sad. You couldn't quite tell whether those were tears, or raindrops, on his face.

His mother came out on the screened-in back porch and hung up some dish towels. "My," she said, "why such a sad face?"

"All my chickens are dead," Donny said. "And now all my popcorn is dead, too." His chin trembled. "So now I suppose I'll *never* have a brother the size of me."

"My goodness," his mother said, "what on earth do chickens and popcorn have to do with a brother the size of you?"

Donny's voice was wavery. "Well, Daddy keeps saying he can't afford any more children. So I thought, if I could sell eggs and popcorn, and chicken fryers — well, I thought I could save up enough money. So we could afford another brother, I mean."

Mother put her arm around his shoulders. "Goodness, if it means *that* much to you, I suppose we could write some more letters to orphanages."

Donny threw his arms around his mother and gave her a big kiss. "Oh, Mama, would you, really?"

Mother smiled. "Remember, I simply said I might write more letters. That doesn't mean we are certain to find a boy, just your age, who needs adopting."

"You just tell them in your letters," Donny said, "that we *aren't* interested in a baby. We want a real *big* boy, for a change. Like me."

"I'll write," Mother said. "We'll see what happens."

Donny and Rufus watched for the mailman every day. A week went by. Then two weeks. Nearly a month went by.

Finally an airmail letter arrived — from faraway Hawaii.

Donny's mother ripped open the envelope. Two pictures fluttered out onto the front porch. Donny picked them up. His eager hopes collapsed, like a punctured balloon.

"These are pictures of two little *girls!*" Donny said, disappointed. "Is this all they've got? No big boys?"

Mother was reading the letter. "It seems that these are the two oldest children they have, at present. One little girl is named Elaine. She is five years old, so that makes her the same age as Teddy, Laura, and Susan."

"But that's not fair!" Donny said. "They all have so many the size of them, already."

Mother turned to the next page. "And the other little girl is Diane. She is just four, so that makes her the same age as Rita. The lady who writes this letter says she hopes we can adopt both of them."

Donny took Rufus and went around the church to his hide-out. Down there in the dimness, he sat with his arm around his dog.

"Those two little girls aren't old enough for me to have fun with," Donny said. "They aren't any bigger than all the rest."

49

Rufus snuggled his cold nose into Donny's hand, and wagged his stubby tail.

"Mama hasn't talked it over with Daddy yet," Donny said. "But I just know she's going to adopt those two girls. I just *know* it. *Why* can't they find just one boy the right size of me?"

Diane   *Elaine*

4. The Airplane

AT LAST all arrangements had been made. The two new girls, Elaine and Diane, were flying from Hawaii by airplane. Soon they would be part of the family, too.

All the children were excited on the day they drove down to the big airport in San Francisco. Even Donny was excited, going to the airport. None of the children had ever been to an airport before.

Daddy parked the station wagon in the airport parking lot. The children jumped out, wide-eyed.

There were rows of shiny airplanes parked along the flying field — all sizes of airplanes. A big plane was warming up its motors with a loud roar, the propellers spinning slow, then fast. A giant stratocruiser was taking off down the runway, slowly lifting itself into the air.

Donny saw a silver speck in the sky. It was coming closer.

"Look, maybe that's the plane our new sisters are on," he said.

Everybody watched it come closer and closer. Now it was very big, as it circled slowly overhead. At last it was coming in straight, rolling down the runway. It taxied up to the door of the waiting room. Men pushed giant stairs up to the airplane door. People started coming down.

"Yes," his mother said, "I think you were right, Donny."

Two small girls were coming down from the plane. They both had big brown eyes and dark brown hair. They had on new, matching coats, and shiny patent-leather shoes. They looked lonely, and lost.

The family crowded around the girls. Mother knelt down and put her arms around them.

"Hello, girls," she said, and she gave each of them a smile and a kiss. "I'm your new mother."

Elaine smiled shyly, and dimples flashed in her cheeks. "Hello, Mommy. I'm Elaine."

Diane threw her arms around Mother, and she didn't look quite so lonely any more. "Are you really our very *own* mommy?" she asked. "Really and always?"

Mother hugged them both again. "Really and always," she said. "And here is your new daddy. *He* is for always, too."

Daddy held out his arms. Diane ran into his arms, and he threw her up into the air and caught her. Diane laughed. Then Elaine pulled on Daddy's coat and said, "Throw *me* up, too, Daddy."

"Now I want you girls to meet your new sisters," Mother said. "This chubby girl with the pretty brown hair is Laura. This girl with the yellow hair and blue

53

eyes is Susie. And this black-haired girl is Rita."

"You have some new brothers, too," Daddy said. "This littlest boy is Alex, and he is just learning to walk. The next bigger boy is Timmy, and the one older than that is Teddy. And the biggest boy of all is *Donny*."

Diane and Elaine smiled shyly at Donny, and he couldn't help smiling back.

Some more passengers came down from the plane, and Elaine called out to them, excited and happy, "*We've* got a mommy *and* a daddy now!"

"Plenty sisters, too," Diane added. "And plenty brothers!"

The next day the two new girls watched Donny fix a pan of dog food for Rufus.

"Oooh, I *like* this doggie," Diane said. "Can I have this doggie for my very own doggie?"

"Oh, no!" Donny said, shocked. "Rufus is my very best *friend*. You don't give away your very best friend."

Diane pointed to the dish of dog food. "Well, then, can I feed him his dinner?"

Donny shook his head solemnly. "No, you see —
just his *owner* is supposed to feed him. I feed him
every day, and that's the way he knows he belongs to
me. If *you* gave him his dinner, then after a while he
would think he belonged to *you*. So that's why I always
feed him myself."

"Oh," Diane said. She looked disappointed.

Donny gave Rufus his dinner, and patted the dog's
shiny rusty-red fur. "You two can stay here and watch
Rufus eat his dinner, if you want. I'm going to bring
you a surprise."

Donny went into his room, and came out with two
stuffed toys. "I'm getting too big to keep these around,
anyway," he said. He handed Diane a toy cocker
spaniel with a furry red body, like Rufus. The toy had
black shoe-button eyes, and a red flannel tongue stick-
ing out. He even had long, floppy, curly ears like
Rufus.

"Is this for me?" Diane said. "I never had such a
pretty-ful toy, all my own. Do I get to keep it?"

"Sure," Donny said generously. Then he took the

other toy, a big brown Teddy bear, and put it into
Elaine's arms.

Elaine's eyes opened wide. "Oh, I *like* this Teddy
bear," she said. "Do I get to keep it, too?"

Donny nodded.

"You're nice," Elaine said. "Just like a big boy who
lived near us, in Hawaii."

Donny looked interested. "Are there many boys the
size of me, over in Hawaii?"

Elaine and Diane nodded.

"Can they be adopted, too?" Donny asked. "Like
you?"

Both girls looked at each other, and shrugged. They
were not sure just what "adopted" meant.

"I guess so," Diane said.

"Will you excuse me?" Donny said. "I just got an
idea."

Rufus followed Donny around the church, and down
into the hide-out.

"How am I going to get to Hawaii?" Donny asked
his dog. "If I could only get over there, I could look

around for *myself*." His arm went around Rufus. "I'll bet *I* could find a boy my size, if I once got over there."

A big horsefly came buzzing past Donny's nose, heading out of the dimness toward the light. Rufus jumped and snapped at it, but he missed.

"I've *got* it!" Donny said. "I'll build an airplane!" He put his arm around his dog. "I know that sounds hard, but I bet I can do it. I read about the Wright brothers in school. *They* made their first plane out of scraps of things, and bicycle wheels, and stuff. Why can't I?"

Late that night, in his bed, Donny thought about it. When he arose in the morning, he knew what he was going to do.

After breakfast, he gathered his sisters and brothers around him.

"Hey, kids," Donny told them solemnly, "I'm going to build an airplane."

"A real airplane?" Timmy wanted to know. "A really real airplane?"

"Sure," Donny said. He hunted up some paper and pencil, climbed up by the dining-room table, and started drawing plans, filling his papers with sketches. "This has got to be planned just right," he murmured. "If you want things to work, you've got to plan them right."

"You mean it'll really fly?" Rita asked.

"Why not?" Donny said. "Now, you little kids stay back and don't bother me. I've got a lot of work to do."

When the planning was done, he stuffed the papers into the hip pocket of his jeans. His brothers and sisters followed him outside, where he began to gather his materials.

Donny found some apple boxes stacked behind the garage, some lumber on the scrap pile, some old wheels from a broken doll buggy. He gathered together some string, some wire, and a can of nails.

"Can people ride in it?" Rita wanted to know.

"Of course," Donny said, hammering.

The children started jumping up and down, begging for turns to ride.

"Don't get excited," Donny said. "Sooner or later, you'll all get a ride."

"How many can fit in it?" Teddy asked.

"Well, it all depends," Donny said, "on the size I make it."

"Make it big enough for all of us to ride at once," little Timmy hollered.

"Yes, yes!" Teddy, Rita, Elaine, Laura, Susan, and Diane all echoed. Alex didn't talk very much yet, but he clapped his little hands in all the excitement.

"All right," Donny agreed. "I'll make it big enough for everybody to all go at once."

"Where will we fly?" Teddy wanted to know.

"How would you like to go to Hawaii?" Donny said.

"Oh, boy," Diane said. "We can say hello at our other house, where me and Elaine used to stay — before we had any family here."

"Is Mama going?" Timmy asked.

"We'll take her next time," Donny whispered. "This time we're going to be *care*free."

"The lady on *our* plane gave us food to eat," Elaine said.

"We'll pack up some sandwiches," Donny said. "We can eat those while we're up in the air."

"How about when we get there?" Teddy asked. "We'll be hungry again."

"Don't worry," Diane said. "We'll eat pineapples. And pick bananas off the trees."

"And coconuts," Donny said. "And we'll drink nothing but coconut milk."

"How will we get the coconuts open?" Timmy asked.

"We'll get a hatchet," Susie said, "and hatch them open. Don't worry."

At noontime they stopped to have a picnic under the tree. Donny made some peanut-butter and lettuce sandwiches in the house, and brought them out.

"Today we drink cow's milk," he said. "Just think, by tomorrow we'll all be drinking coconut milk."

"These are good sammiches," Laura told Donny.

Timmy, staring at his sandwich, murmured, "Hey, there's a bug on my lettuce."

"Couldn't be," Donny said. "I washed it good." Then he told the other children, "I'll have to train one of you to be my navigator."

"I want to be the alligator," Diane said.

"There is too a bug on my lettuce," Timmy said. But nobody was listening to Timmy.

"Not alligator," Donny told Diane. *"Navigator."*

"There is too a bug," Timmy told Donny.

"It's probably just a speck of dirt," Donny told Timmy. Then he said, "I guess I'll have to read the maps myself, because I'm the only one who can read."

Timmy was still staring at his sandwich. "How can it be dirt, when it's *crawling?*" he asked.

After lunch, some changes had to be made. Donny found a big crate which once had held a new chest of drawers. Donny began to saw out windows along the side.

"This will make a good cabin," Donny said. "It will hold more people than those little apple boxes I was using."

Rita shook her head. "I'm not going," she said. "It might get bust."

"Not a chance," Donny told her. "Not the way I make it."

"Yes," Rita said, tossing her jet-black hair. "But what

if the bottom falls out, right when we're over the ocean?"

"Don't worry so much," Donny said. "This will be sturdy."

"I don't trust it," Rita decided, running off on her slim brown legs that never seemed to touch the ground. "I'm going to catch me some grasser-hoppers." Suddenly she jumped back. "Hey, what's this bug? Hey, Donny, what's this bug? Is it poison?" Her fingers were ready to catch it if it wasn't.

"That's a dragonfly," Donny said.

Timmy, studying the insect, said, "What does it drag? I don't see it draggin' anything."

"What do you kids want to monkey around with dragonflies for?" Donny asked. "You just stick around me, and you can fly better than any little old bug."

"When we're going over the ocean, I'm not going to look out the windows," Susie said. "I don't want to get dizzy and fall out. I can't swim."

Teddy said, "Hadn't we better practice a little bit, before we try such a long trip?"

64

"We might," Donny said. "If we get through early tonight, we might fly around the house for a bit, first."

Late that afternoon, Teddy decided not to go. "You haven't got any motor in it," he said, his brown face screwed up as he studied Donny's contraption. "I don't see how it's going to work."

"It's going to work, isn't it, kids?" Donny said.

Everybody gave loud cheers, except Rita, who was off bug-hunting.

"Anyway," Teddy said, "I still think I'll stay home. I got some other things to do."

"Hey, you can't back out now," Donny begged, scratching his blond head. "I'm *depending* on you."

"What for?" Teddy's large brown eyes were wary.

"To help me fly it."

Teddy frowned, perplexed. "How?"

"Well, I was going to have you sit in the middle, and flap the wings," Donny said. "I was going to get Timmy to sit behind you, and work the tail part."

"That's not the way airplanes fly," Teddy said. "They

have motors, and the motors make the propellers go round."

"Not *this* airplane," Donny said. "It's going to fly like a *bird*. Birds don't have motors. They flap their wings."

"I still don't think it'll work," Teddy said. "Who ever heard of *boys* making real airplanes?"

"Everything has to be invented for the first time," Donny said patiently. "I'm trying to invent a simple sort of airplane that boys *can* make." He leaned down, and his blue eyes looked into Teddy's brown ones. "Boys can make *toy* airplanes that really fly, can't they?"

"I guess so," Teddy admitted.

"Well," Donny said, "this is the same thing, only bigger."

When it grew dark, Mother came to the door and called, "Time for supper!"

"Do we have to?" Donny said. "I'm getting pretty close to finished."

"Why don't you all come in and have a good hot supper?" Mother said. "After such a day of hard work, you'll need your sleep, too. You can finish your plane in the morning, when it is light again."

"Well," Donny agreed, "I still *do* have a lot of work to do on it."

So everyone went in, ate the hearty supper, and scooted off to bed. They chattered about the fun they were going to have on the trip, until they finally fell asleep.

In the night, a storm blew up. The play yard turned into a small lake. Donny's airplane fell apart into a pile of boxes, boards, nails, string, wire and doll-buggy wheels.

In the morning the children ran to the windows and pressed their noses against the glass, staring out at the rain.

Donny felt very sad. Now he couldn't fly to Hawaii, and maybe he would *never* find a brother his size. He sighed. "I suppose it's a good thing it fell apart now, and not when we were about a thousand miles up in the sky."

"Are you going to build another one, Donny?" his brothers and sisters wanted to know.

"I don't know," Donny said. "Maybe I'll wait till next year when I'm older, and I can learn how to make a more *durable* one out of metal. That is," Donny added sadly, "if I don't have too much sense by then."

Donny

5. The Price of a Brother

ONE DAY, Donny sat down at the desk in his room and wrote a letter. When it was all finished, he took it to his mother.

"Can you send this letter for me?" he asked.

"Send it where?" Mother wanted to know.

"To the lady who owns the orphanage."

"Which orphanage?"

"*Any* orphanage. Any place that's got boys to

adopt, just the right size of me. Here, you can read it."

His mother read the letter. It read:

Dere Lady,

I would like a bother 9 years old, my father made me a room, it has a desk, a doubble desk, cowboy Bunk Bed, Cowboy and Indian wallpaper, two rugs a table some blocks a car and other toys so you see theres lots of room for a new bother.

Donald Doss

"*Bother?*" Mother smiled. "Is that what you want, a bother?"

"*Brother*," Donny said. "Maybe I wrote the letter in a kind of hurry, and my spelling isn't too good. But if you can put it in a letter and send it some place, I think the lady will know what I mean."

Mother folded up the letter. She put her arm around Donny. "You never give up, do you, son? You must want a brother your size more than anything."

"Yes," Donny said wistfully, "more than anything."

"I'll talk to Daddy," Mother said. "We'll see."

Several weeks later, Mother took a letter out of the mailbox. She looked at the address up in the corner before she opened it.

"Hmm," she said. "It looks as if this is from that orphanage I wrote to."

Donny came running over, Rufus at his heels. "Have they got a boy? One the size of me?"

Mother read the letter. "No, I'm afraid you are going to be disappointed again. They have a little Indian boy, but he is just a baby. Even younger than Alex. His name is Gregory, and they hope we can adopt him."

"Oh, Mother," Donny said in despair. "You won't take him, will you? He's too little!"

"Perhaps we may decide to take him, anyway," Mother said. "This baby needs a home, and we can't turn him down, can we?"

Donny ran around the church and crawled down into his hide-out. Rufus followed him in, and sat down beside Donny. Donny put his arm around his dog.

"I suppose I should just give up hope," he said sadly. "But I just *won't*."

A few weeks later, Donny followed his mother out to the mailbox. "When are you going to the orphanage to get the new baby?" he asked.

"Next week, I think," Mother said.

"Do you suppose you might get another letter from the orphanage before that?" Donny asked. "Maybe saying we didn't need to take the baby, because they'd found a big boy my size?" ·

Mother pulled out the mail. "There's little chance of that, I'm afraid." She took the top letter from the pile. "Well, look at this! This first letter is for *you*. Looks like Grandma's handwriting."

Donny and his mother sat down on the front porch and opened their letters.

"Hey, look!" Donny said happily. "*Three* dollars!" He took out a birthday card. On the back was a note.

Dear Donny —

I just returned from my trip, and I noticed that I missed your birthday while I was gone. So here is a late birthday present, for you to spend as you choose.

Love,
Grandma

"Whoopee!" Donny said.

Mother finished reading her letter, and smiled. "Now maybe you will *really* have something to *whoopee* about."

"Why?" Donny said, counting his crisp new dollar bills again.

"Your wish has come true, after all!" Mother said. "I have here a letter from the orphanage where I am going to get baby Gregory. And guess what?"

"They have a boy the size of *me?*" Donny said, hardly daring to hope.

Mother nodded. "That's right. His name is Richard, and he is just exactly your age! Not only that, but now they also have a girl named Dorothy, and *she* is just exactly your age, too."

"Gosh!" Donny said. "Am I lucky!"

"I just had another idea," Mother said. "How would you like to go for a long trip on the train, to help me bring Richard and Dorothy and baby Gregory home?"

"Oh, boy!" Donny said, giving his mother a hug and a kiss.

"You can be a real help on the trip home," Mother said. "The lady at the orphanage writes that both Richard and Dorothy are quite shy and lonely. When she asked them about going away to be adopted, they seemed to be afraid of the idea. Your job will be to make friends with them. Then they won't be so afraid to go home with perfect strangers, to a strange house far away."

"Oh, I'll do that," Donny said. "I'll be the friendliest boy you ever saw."

Finally the day came when Donny's suitcase was packed, and Mother's suitcase was packed.

Daddy drove them to the train. All Donny's little brothers and sisters were chattering in the back seat.

"Hurry back, Mama," they all said. "Hurry back, Donny. We'll miss you."

"I'll miss all of you," Donny said generously.

On the train, Donny was almost too excited to watch out of the windows. He could hear the wheels going *clickety-click, clickety-clack*. It seemed as if they were saying, "A new brother for me, a new brother for me!"

After a day and a night, riding in the coach seats of the train, they got off at a big station.

"Is the orphanage here?" Donny asked.

"No," his mother said. "We have to walk down that street until we come to the big hotel in the next block. We have to wait there for nearly two hours, to catch a bus going north."

So Donny and his mother picked up their suitcases, and started walking down the street.

"I've got my three dollars in my wallet," Donny said. "I'd like to spend it for something on this trip."

His mother nodded. "It is yours to spend."

"Just think," Donny said, "three dollars will buy — " he stopped to figure a minute — "*thirty* double-scoop ice-cream cones!" He figured again, his brow wrinkled. "Or it would buy *sixty* candy bars!" He scratched his blond head, and figured again. "Or three *hundred* sticks of gum. *Whew!*"

They passed a bookstore, right next to the hotel. Donny stopped to look in the window.

"Hey, look!" he cried out, pointing. "There's Rufus! Right there on that book."

His mother looked. Sure enough, there was a large, thin book. On the jacket was a red cocker spaniel. He looked just like Donny's dog.

When they walked into the hotel lobby, Mother put their suitcases by a writing desk.

"I think I'll write a note to Daddy," she said. "Then perhaps we can get a drink of milk and a sweet roll while we wait for our bus."

"May I go next door," Donny said, "while you write that letter? I want to look in the bookstore once more."

"Go ahead," Mother said. "But don't go any farther away than that."

"I won't," Donny said, and hurried out of the hotel. He stood in front of the bookstore window, looking at the book with Rufus on it. Finally he went inside.

A gray-haired lady came up. "Can I help you?"

"Yes," Donny said. He walked to the door and pointed in the window. "How much is that book with the cocker spaniel on the front?"

The lady opened the back of the window, and

76

handed him the book. "This one would come to just two dollars and ninety cents," she said.

Donny opened the book and looked through the pages.

"It is a fine dog story," the lady said. "If you like dogs, I know you would like that story."

"I do like dogs, very much," Donny said. "Especially one dog, who looks just like this. His name is Rufus, and I like him better than anything I've got."

Donny laid the book down and pulled out his wallet. He took out a snapshot of Rufus, a little worn from carrying around. "See," he said proudly. "This is my Rufus."

The lady nodded. "Yes, there *is* a remarkable resemblance to the dog on the book, isn't there?"

Donny put his picture back and took out his three dollars. Now there was nothing left in his wallet except the worn snapshot of his dog. Donny looked at the money in his hand.

"I could buy three hundred sticks of gum," he said. "Or sixty candy bars. Or thirty double-decker ice-cream cones." He smiled at the lady, and shrugged.

"But after I ate them, I wouldn't have anything left."

He handed her his three dollars. "A book I can always keep, forever and ever."

"That is pretty clear thinking for a boy your size," the lady said. She put his book into a new white sack, and gave him back a dime.

Donny looked at the dime in his hand. It would be nice to buy two candy bars, or a double-decker ice-cream cone, or ten sticks of chewing gum. But he would not have had this wonderful book if Grandma hadn't remembered him on his birthday. Now Grandma's birthday was coming next week. He ought to remember *her* birthday, while he still had some money.

"Do you have a nice birthday card for ten cents?" he asked. "It's for Grandma, so I'd like a nice one."

"I have just the thing," the lady said. She went to the counter and came back with a card that said, HAPPY BIRTHDAY TO MY GRANDMOTHER. It had roses and violets painted all around it.

Donny smiled. "That's a fine one. I'll take that."

The lady put the card into a small white sack, and Donny gave her his last dime. Then he hurried back to the hotel.

"See what I bought with my three dollars?" Donny said. He showed his mother the birthday card. "Can you put this in your suitcase, and save it for me until Grandma's birthday, next week?"

Then he carefully took his book out of the new white sack. "See?" he said. "It's a story about a dog, and he looks just like Rufus." He smiled. "I'm going to keep this book for years and *years*."

"That is a good thing to spend your money on," Mother said. "Books make good friends."

"Just like dogs," Donny said.

Finally the bus came, and they rode for half a day. When the bus arrived at the town, Mother and Donny got off. Then they boarded a small city bus.

"Do you really mean we're almost there?" Donny said eagerly. "I can hardly wait. What do you suppose my new brother looks like?"

Donny soon found out.

First the lady at the orphanage took Mother and Donny to the nursery, to see baby Gregory. He was a chubby little papoose, with brown skin and big brown eyes.

"This baby is a full-blooded Blackfoot Indian," the lady told them.

"*Black*foot?" Donny said. He looked at the chubby baby in the crib, waving his pink fists, and kicking his bare feet in the air. "But the bottoms of his feet aren't black! They're *pink*."

Mother picked up the baby and hugged him. "Black-foot is just the name of his Indian tribe," Mother said. "Isn't he a darling?"

Next they went to see Dorothy. Dorothy had curly chestnut-brown hair, and hazel-blue eyes. She was pretty, and very bashful. Mother put her arms around her.

"Would you like to come and live with us?" Donny asked.

Dorothy began to look frightened. "I — I don't know."

Donny looked at her, and he didn't know what he could say to cheer her up. He thought what it would be like to be in an orphanage, and go home to live with strange people. *What* could he do, to give her something to be happy about?

His book was still there, under his arm. He could feel it, hard and flat.

"Do you like to read books?" Donny asked Dorothy.

Dorothy nodded, shyly.

"Do you like books about dogs?" Donny asked.

Dorothy looked interested. "Oh, yes. I like books about *dogs* or *horses* best of any kind of books at all."

"Have you got any books of your own?" Donny asked.

Dorothy looked shy again. She shook her head.

"You *ought* to have some books of your own," Donny said. "Here, take this and write your name in it." He handed her his book. "This will be your very first book. After you have some birthdays and Christmases at our house, you'll probably have a *lot* of books of your very own."

Dorothy pulled the book out of the white sack, and she smiled when she saw the picture of Rufus on the front.

"That's really pretty," she said, and her hazel-blue eyes didn't look so afraid any more. She looked at Donny as though she would be glad to go home, and be part of his family.

A little later, Mother and Donny went to see Richard.

Richard looked even more shy than Dorothy. He had brown eyes and freckles, and he wore glasses. Mother had told Donny that Richard was half Indian, but Donny thought he looked like any American boy.

"Golly, you're just the same size as me," Donny crowed. "Hey, wait till you see our room — and wait till you see our bunk beds. Do you want to sleep in the top bunk or the bottom bunk?"

Richard didn't have much to say. He just hung his head and mumbled when Donny asked him questions.

Later, the orphanage lady said, "This has all been pretty sudden for Richard. Maybe by the time he has all his things packed, in the morning, he may feel a little happier about going."

The next morning, Donny and his mother went to the orphanage office. Dorothy was waiting for them, with her suitcase all packed. She held her new book in her arms. She was still shy, but she looked happy about going.

"Would you like to go with me to the nursery?" Mother asked Dorothy. "I'm going to pick up your new baby brother. His name is *Gregory*."

Dorothy nodded. "All right, Mama," she said shyly.

Mother looked at Donny. "While we get the baby, maybe you would like to go up to the boys' dormitory and see if Richard is all ready to go."

"Okay," Donny said eagerly. "I'll go see."

The orphanage lady showed Donny where the boys' dormitory was. Donny went up, and found Richard sitting on the bed, with his head in his hands. His suitcase was empty on the floor. Everything that had been packed in it was dumped out on the bed, beside him.

"Hey, aren't you ready to go?" Donny wanted to know.

Richard didn't move.

"Don't you want to go?" Donny asked.

Richard shook his head slowly, back and forth, without looking up.

Donny sat on the bed beside him. "Well, gee," he said, "you've *got* to come. You just don't know how much fun we're going to have. We've got a real nice family. We've got *eight* more kids waiting for you, back at home. And a *swell* daddy."

Richard shook his head.

Donny felt helpless. What could he do to cheer Richard up? Maybe if he *didn't* cheer him up, Richard might refuse to go home with them. If Richard wouldn't come, Donny might never have a brother his size.

"Do you like dogs?" Donny said.

Richard looked up, and nodded, warily.

"Do you want to see a picture of *my* dog?" Donny said. He took his wallet from his hip pocket. Carefully he pulled out the worn snapshot, holding it like a treasure. "That's my dog, Rufus."

"I never had a dog all my own," Richard said sadly. "I always wanted a dog all my own, but I never had one."

Donny thought a moment, and he swallowed hard. This was the hardest thing he had ever had to do, but he knew he must do it.

"Well, you've got yourself a dog now!" Donny said, and he tried to smile big, as if he were completely happy. He put his wallet back into his pocket again, empty. Then he laid the snapshot in Richard's hand.

"You can have his picture, too," Donny said. "He's a registered cocker spaniel, sort of a rusty red." He swallowed again. "He — he'll be your best friend."

Richard looked and looked at the picture, as if he couldn't believe it. "You mean this is going to be *my* dog? My very own dog, all my own?"

"That's right," Donny said. "As soon as we get home,

he'll be waiting for you. So we'd better get your stuff back into your suitcase, or we'll miss our bus."

Donny started piling the things on the bed into the suitcase. "Does all this stuff go?"

Richard nodded, and started helping Donny.

"How will my dog know he belongs to me?" Richard asked, stuffing all the socks into one corner of the suitcase.

"Because you will get to feed him," Donny said. "He knows he belongs to the one who feeds him every day. He's a very smart dog."

"Oh," Richard said. They put the last of the jeans in, and closed the suitcase.

"I'll carry it," Richard said. He looked straight at Donny, and he smiled, slowly, for the first time. Donny could tell that he was going to like this new brother very much.

"I'm glad I've got myself a dog," Richard said. "I think I'm going to like it at my new house, after all."

They went downstairs. Mother and the new big sister, Dorothy, were waiting. Mother was carrying the new baby brother.

"We're ready to go home now," Donny said, linking his arm with Richard's. "Me, and my new brother the size of me, we're ready to go home now."

Rita

Teddy

Laura

Elaine

Susan

Alex

Diane

Gregory

Timmy

Dorothy

Donny

Richard